CRAZY CLASSICS

Frankenstein 2.0

Une histoire réinterprétée par

Roger Morris

et illustrée par Euan Cook

didier

... et encore merci à Soizic Cornet et Caroline Moreau, dont l'enthousiasme et la connaissance des élèves ont aidé cet ouvrage à trouver la bonne altitude !

Direction artistique : Mandy Norman
Maquette intérieure et composition : Becky Chilcott
Édition : Catherine Laurent, Sandrine Paniel
Enregistrements : Studio Corby

« Le photocopillage, c'est l'usage abusif et collectif de la photocopie sans autorisation des auteurs et des éditeurs.
Largement répandu dans les établissements d'enseignement, le photocopillage menace l'avenir du livre, car il met en danger son équilibre économique. Il prive les auteurs d'une juste rémunération. En dehors de l'usage privé du copiste, toute reproduction totale ou partielle de cet ouvrage est interdite. »
« La loi du 11 mars 1957 n'autorisant, au terme des alinéas 2 et 3 de l'article 41, d'une part, que les copies ou reproductions strictement réservées à l'usage privé du copiste et non destinées à une utilisation collective » et, d'autre part, que les analyses et les courtes citations dans un but d'exemple et d'illustration, « toute représentation ou reproduction intégrale, ou partielle, faite sans le consentement de l'auteur ou de ses ayants droit ou ayants cause, est illicite. » (alinéa 1er de l'article 40) – « Cette représentation ou reproduction, par quelque procédé que ce soit, constituerait donc une contrefaçon sanctionnée par les articles 425 et suivants du Code pénal. »

© Les Éditions Didier, Paris, 2014 – ISBN 978-2-278-07939-1 – ISSN 2271-7269
Dépôt légal : 7939/02 – Achevé d'imprimer en France en mai 2016 par Jouve

paper planes *teens*

*Une collection imaginée avec humour,
enthousiasme et provocation par* Rupert Morgan

Tous les titres que vous pourrez *enfin* lire en anglais !

A1→A2
- What is Brian? *Rupert Morgan*
- Welcome to Star School, *Michaela Morgan*
- Panic at Star School, *Michaela Morgan*
- Star School on Tour, *Michaela Morgan*

A2→B1
- Macbeth and the Creature from Hell, *Roger Morris*
- Romeo and Juliet in Las Vegas, *Rupert Morgan*
- Bubonic Britain, *Philippa Boston*
- Deadly Jobs, *Philippa Boston*
- Blitz Britain, *Philippa Boston*
- Killer Sports, *Philippa Boston*

B1→B2
- Frankenstein 2.0, *Roger Morris*
- Facebook Dracula, *Peter Flynn*
- Live Fast, Die Young, *Rupert Morgan*
- Rock Rebels, *Rupert Morgan*

Sun, Sand and Death

'Victor!'

I was in the lake, trying to stay cool, when I heard my name. Standing up, I felt the sun's heat on my shoulders as I scanned the beach.

Elizabeth was signalling to me. Something was wrong.

I ran across the sand as fast as possible.

'It's your mum,' said Elizabeth when I got to her.

I looked down at Mum, lying on her beach towel. Her face was burned by the sun and she was not moving. I took off her sunglasses – her eyes were open, but there was no life in them.

'Mum!' I cried out, desperately trying to wake her up. It was no good – she did not answer. I fell to my knees on the hot sand and began to cry.

Elizabeth reached out a hand to comfort me. 'Victor, I'm so sorry.'

At that moment, I saw my father coming back with my little brother Billy. Dad had four melting ice creams in his hands. Billy was eating the fifth.

When Dad saw my face, he dropped the ice creams and ran to my mother. He was calm. He felt for her pulse. Then, as Billy also started to cry, he tried to call the emergency SolarCopter on his PsyCom.

Other people on the beach came to see if they could help. A man who said he was a doctor tried to revive her. Eventually, he shook his head at my father, saying 'There might still be a chance for her if the SolarCopter gets here fast enough.'

But it didn't. That winter was the hottest on record. People were dying from the heat all over the place and the emergency services had too much work.

My father started to lift her body. 'Help me get her into the water, Victor.'

'What?' I was confused, frightened. But I wanted to believe that my father could help her, that there was some way of saving my mother.

'Our only hope is to keep her cool until we can take her to the Institute. A hospital can't help her now. We have to look after her our way.'

Our way. The Frankenstein way.

The Frankenstein Way

The SolarCopter carried us home to Mont Blanc. Me, my father, Billy and Elizabeth. And my mother.

Mont Blanc, the White Mountain that was no longer white. My father chose it as the location for his business because of all the snow and ice. It was a marketing idea. But these days Mont Blanc was just a big black rock.

Let me explain. The family business is cryonics: the Future Life Institute. Maybe you have heard of it.

I remember when my father first told me about cryonics:

'Cry what?' I said.

'Cryonics, Victor. It's the science of keeping dead people in a deep freeze until a day in the future when you can bring them back to life. The idea is that medical science will one day advance so much that they can be cured* of whatever killed them.'

'How do you bring the bodies back to life, Dad?'

'Ah! That is a very good question, Victor. No one has ever done it. Yet.'

Soon after that, Elizabeth came to live with us. She was the daughter of some family friends who had died in a car accident.

We were the same age, and she fascinated me from the moment she arrived. Her sad beauty, touched by tragedy. As I saw her crying, I thought to myself: *If only we could bring her parents back to life, Elizabeth would not be sad any more.*

Now, in the SolarCopter, our positions had changed: she smiled gently at me, her eyes full of sympathy and concern.

*cure: *guérir / soigner*

The Future Life Institute

As we approached Mont Blanc, we could see the pyramid-shape of The Future Life Institute. The SolarCopter landed on the roof and closed its solar panels like a giant insect.

'Elizabeth, can you take Billy for his bath, please?' said my father. 'Victor, I need you to help me.'

We put my mother's body on a trolley and pushed it into the elevator.

'Level 6,' he said.

I pressed the button, and the elevator took us down past our living quarters into the lower levels of the Institute.

The dead bodies were stored vertically in glass capsules. Families liked to see their loved ones when they came to visit.

As we pushed my mother past the bodies, the soft white light inside each capsule gave the illusion that the dead people were coming toward us from the icy mist*.

The dead did not trouble me. The only part of the Institute that I didn't like was Level 12, where we placed the clients who were not rich enough to freeze their entire bodies. On Level 12, there were only heads.

*mist: *brume*

My father opened the door of an empty freezer unit. I felt the blast of cold air on my face.

'Cold, isn't it?' he whispered. 'Minus 200 degrees.'

Icy smoke drifted out as we put my mother inside. I saw that my father was crying as he closed the door.

'One day, Dad,' I promised him. 'One day, we'll bring her back.'

The School of Sleep

Some weeks later, my father called me into his office.

'Victor, I have made a decision. I am going to retire* from the business.'

He looked out of the window at the valley. Where before it was white with an immense glacier, now the valley was dark and sombre. 'I want to enjoy the rest of my life.'

'What do you mean, Dad? Are you sick?'

My father smiled sadly. 'Me? No! But the planet is sick, Victor. Suppose that, one day, we discover how to reanimate the dead: will they want to return to a dying world?'

I'd never heard my father speak like this. Preoccupied by my own sadness, I had not realised

---

*retire: prendre sa retraite

how much my mother's death had affected him.

'It is time for you to manage the Institute, Victor,' he said.

My father opened a drawer in his desk and produced a NeuroSyringe.

He placed it on my temple*. The entry of the nano-implant was not painful, but I immediately felt a strange sensation in my head. I began to see flashes of numbers and letters.

'I've just injected you with a BiblioFile containing my library of books and papers on cryonics.

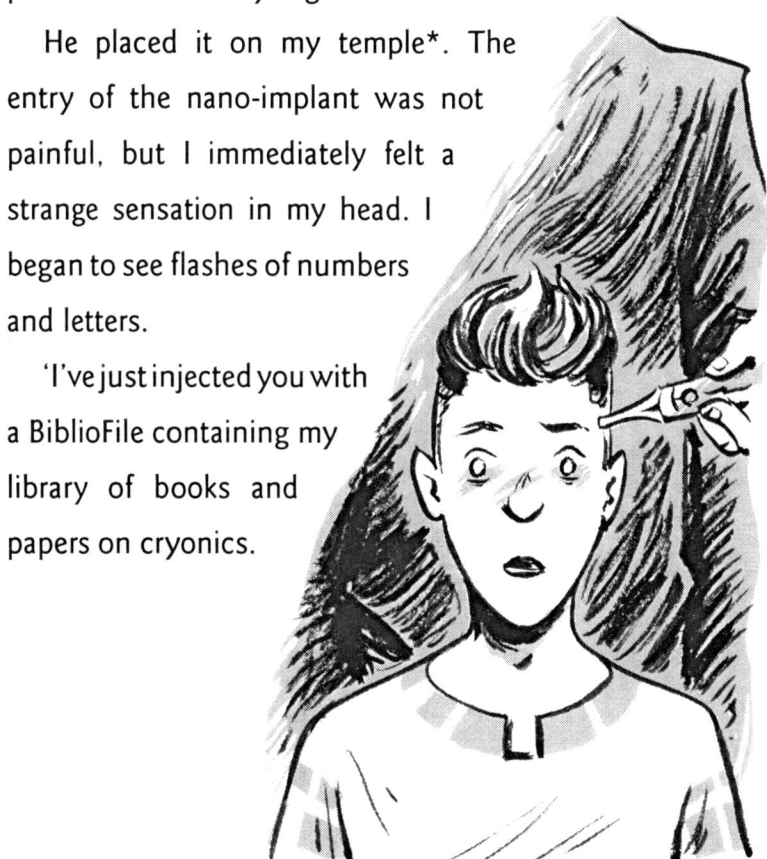

*temple: *tempe*

You will need several months, possibly even years, to absorb all this information. But, eventually, you will know everything there is to know on the subject.'

I was a little unstable on my feet, as if drunk* with knowledge.

'The BiblioFile also records information,' said Dad. 'It will keep a copy of your personal research and your thoughts. I'm sure it will make fascinating reading one day!'

The fastest way to absorb information from a BiblioFile is to sleep a lot. I began to go to bed early each day and sleep until lunch. I learned fast.

In the afternoons, I jogged along the corridors of the Institute. As I ran past the cryonic capsules, the dead watched me from their icy mist, silently encouraging me.

Soon! I whispered to them as I passed.

*drunk: ivre

18

Till Death Do Us Part

One day I called the company accountant, Henri Clerval, to my office.

'Henri, I want to look at the accounts.'

'Of course, Victor. Is there anything in particular you want to know?'

'Let's be honest, Henri – this is a strange business. All of our clients are dead.'

'That's the nature of our work, Victor.'

'And tell me, Henri – how do the dead pay their bills?'

'Some... better than others,' he answered. 'It depends how rich they were when they died.'

'And those who were not rich? When there is no more money, what happens to their bodies?'

Henri moved nervously in his chair. He was a

good man. My questions made him uncomfortable. 'Nothing. Your father always...'

'I'm not my father. What do the contracts say?'

'The contracts say the Institute will destroy the body. But your father always believed we should keep their bodies if there was space in the Institute. You never know, someone in their family might pay the bill one day.'

'And as I told you, I'm not my father.'

In the Company of Corpses

My dreams were no longer filled with the information from the BiblioFile. I dreamed, instead, of the future. I dreamed of a world populated by superior beings. Superior beings that I was going to create.

I dreamed of a world that gave homage to me, Victor Frankenstein: the man who had finally conquered Death.

These dreams obsessed me. They inspired in me strange emotions that I could not control. I felt myself changing as my knowledge expanded. I was excited by the power it gave me. I became a monster of ambition and arrogance. I was no longer a man. I was God's equal.

Every afternoon as I ran along the corridors, I looked for good specimens. I wanted men who had died young. When I saw a body I liked, I stopped to look closer. Sometimes, I even talked to the dead person.

'Hello, my friend. And how are you today? What's that? You're cold? Soon you will be warm again. I will put life back into your veins. Yes, that's right. I want your veins. Your lovely, healthy veins.'

They never answered me, of course. They just looked back at me as if I was crazy. Maybe I *was* a little crazy.

'Victor? Who are you talking to?' a voice said behind me one day.

'Elizabeth!' I answered in surprise, 'What are you doing here?'

Elizabeth looked hurt. 'I was looking for you. Do you realise how long it is since we've seen you upstairs?'

'My work is important, Elizabeth.'

'But we're your family, Victor!'

'Yes, I know. Now, if there is nothing else...'

'You want to continue talking to yourself?' she said angrily.

I smiled. 'It helps me to think.'

'I prefer talking to other people. Other *living* people. What I'd really like is to talk to *you* again.' Elizabeth turned and started to walk away.

I called after her. 'Elizabeth! Please! I'm sorry. I didn't mean to...'

She stopped.

'It's just that my work is at a crucial phase.

It won't be long now, I promise. Just be patient a little longer, Elizabeth. That's all I ask.' I gave her my best smile.

She smiled back. 'I have to get back to your father and Billy. You know you're always welcome upstairs for dinner.'

'I can't tonight. But soon… I promise.'

Perfect Pieces

Whenever I found a good body, I checked the accounts. If the client had stopped paying, I transported the body to a secret laboratory I had built in the basement[1] of the Institute.

In order to preserve the bodies I used for my research, the temperature in the lab was glacial. This obliged me to wear thermal clothes and gloves, which made the delicate surgical work more difficult.

Have you ever cut open a corpse and removed the heart? Or the pancreas gland? Or the spinal column[2]?

If you have, you'll know how satisfying it is. The hours passed rapidly.

Every time I removed an organ, I immersed it in a special solution of my invention. This solution

---

1. **basement:** *sous-sol*
2. **spinal column:** *colonne vertébrale*

was essential to the reanimation process, but it produced a strange secondary effect: the body parts became bigger.

Soon I had nearly enough parts to assemble a complete being. And it was going to be a giant.

The only thing I didn't have was the head.

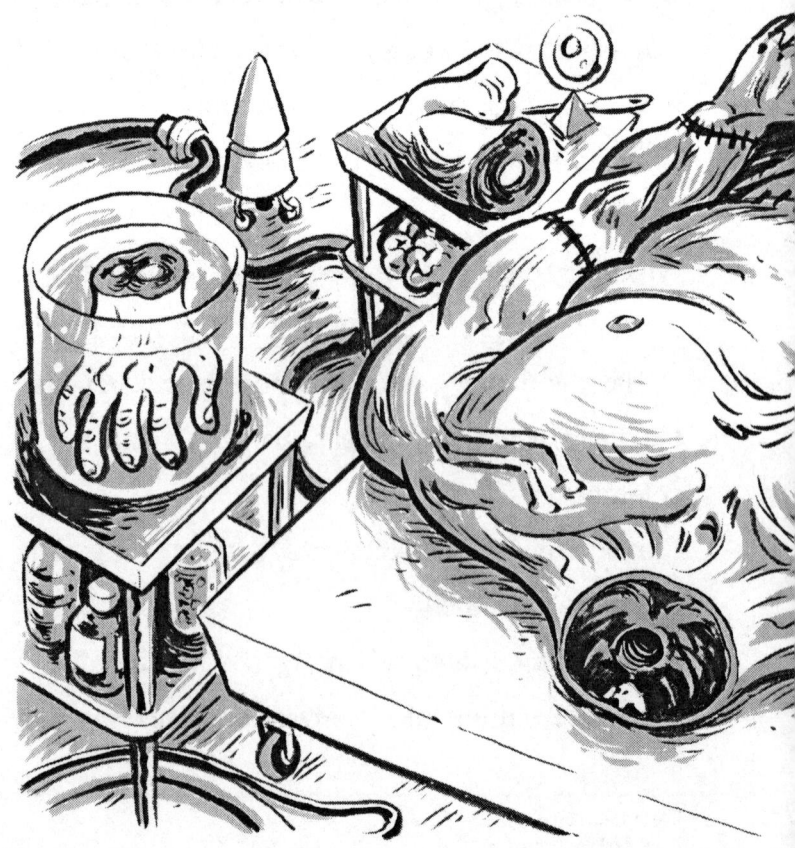

Head-to-Head

I rarely went to Level 12.

I don't know why I had such an irrational fear of the frozen heads. Maybe it was a premonition of the future.

The walls were lined with hundreds of heads, looking at me from the icy mist.

The creature I was constructing was male. So naturally I wanted a male head. And it had to be perfect. He was to be the first of his kind. The world would be looking at him.

'Sorry, you're too old,' I said to one.

'No offence,' I told another, 'but you look like a pig.'

'Eyes too close together, I'm afraid.'

At last I found the perfect specimen. 'Head 247. You're just what I'm looking for.'

It was the head of a handsome young man. His face had a friendly expression. You don't see that often on dead people.

I checked the records. The bills for this client hadn't been paid for over ten years.

I took Head 247 to my secret lab in a refrigerated box. I immersed it in the secret formula.

Unfortunately, the process completely transformed the head. Just like the other body parts, it increased in size. But it did so in an irregular manner.

When it emerged from the solution, it was the ugliest head I had ever seen.

The Creature Lives

My creation lay on a metal table, unmoving, inert. All it needed to come to life was an electrical stimulus. At the push of a button, it would become a living being.

And I would become God's equal.

No doubt, my excitement made me blind. My only thought was that I was about to give life to dead flesh. Nothing else mattered.

In my naiveté, I even fitted a basic language implant into my creation's brain. 'When you wake, we will talk,' I said to him. 'What wonders you will have to tell!'

I pressed the button. The metal table flashed as electricity passed through it.

My creation trembled violently, its arms and legs

jerking in the air. At one point, it even levitated above the metal surface. Then, when the electrical surge stopped, it landed heavily on the table.

I held my breath. The creature did not move.

Then, slowly, its head began to turn towards me.

It... *he* opened his eyes and looked at me. That was the moment when I saw the horror of what I had done. When I saw his horrible, yellow eyes moving with an animation that was impossible in death. But which was not true life either.

The creature opened his mouth and an inhuman sound came out, a cry of anger and pain. *'Please,'* he cried. *'Please help me! It hurts! Everything hurts!'*

A wave of repulsion went through me. I ran from my lab. I ran from the Institute, out into the night. My only thought was to put as much distance as possible between me and the abomination I had created...

The Empty Laboratory

When I eventually found the courage to return to the laboratory, it was empty.

I searched the entire Institute, but there was no sign of the monster. If it had escaped outside, people would see it. There would be something on the news about it. But the day passed with no mention of a hideous giant in the media.

And the next day. And a week. Then months...

I tried to put the creature out of my mind by concentrating on the business. I slept in my office, hardly seeing anyone until one day my father contacted me by PsyCom: 'It would be good to see you. Elizabeth sends her love.'

Elizabeth. It seemed like years since I had seen her. When I joined them upstairs, she looked at me with sad, concerned eyes. 'I've been worried about you, Victor. I care, you know. I care deeply.'

I took her hand and kissed it. 'Yes, I know.'

It was a shock to see my little brother Billy. 'When did you become a *teenager*?'

'You have been too obsessed with your work, Victor,' said my father.

'Well, you'll see more of me from now on, I promise. Hey, Billy, why don't we go on the roof and kick a ball around?'

'I'm sorry, but I can't,' he answered. 'I'm meeting some friends.'

I was sorry to see him go, suddenly realising how

much affection I had for him, but we passed a lovely evening together, just the three of us.

It was after three a.m. that night when my father woke me.

'Victor,' he said gravely, 'Something terrible has happened to Billy.' I felt suddenly cold all over.

11

The Murderer

The police found Billy's body abandoned beside one of the old automobile routes.

He had been strangled*. They recovered some visual information from his neuro-implant and asked my father and me to come to the police station to view it.

Apparently, Billy's killer had worn a mask – a sack with holes cut out for the eyes. I had a terrible premonition. I felt sure I knew who was behind that mask.

'He was probably attacked by someone with mental health problems,' said the police detective. 'Or a drug addict. There's not much information in the neuro-implant, but the killer's eyes are unusual. I'm sorry to have to ask you to do this,

---

*strangled: étranglé

but I'm sure you would remember if you knew this individual...'

He handed over the prints of the memories taken from Billy's implant.

'Those eyes!' I cried out in horror when I saw the picture the policeman gave me.

'Horrible, aren't they?' the policeman said. 'So yellow. So... inhuman.'

12

Father and Son

I had to find the monster and destroy it. But, to my surprise, he found me first: he was waiting for me when I returned to the Institute.

'Hello, Victor.' The words emerged from a mouth with black lips and grey teeth. 'Or should I call you Daddy?'

'There is no genetic connection between us,' I said.

'And yet you gave me life. And then you abandoned me. I was in pain. All that electricity. You... have not been a good father to me.'

I suddenly had an idea. 'I know,' I said. 'I'm sorry. Please... come inside.'

The monster looked at me suspiciously. But I think he wanted to believe. He followed me into the Institute.

I led him to Level 11, where most of the cryonic capsules were empty.

I opened the door of a freezer unit. 'The police are looking for you. If we put you in suspended animation* for a few years, I can reanimate you when it's safer for me to acknowledge you as my creation.'

The monster laughed. The laughter of a creature made from pieces of dead people is a terrifying sound.

'You did not make me an idiot, Victor.'

---

*suspended animation: *hibernation artificielle*

He moved quickly, pushing me inside the capsule and shutting the door.

I was trapped!

The cold was like a thousand icy knives cutting me at once. I felt the blood slow in my veins. My thoughts began to break up. All I wanted to do was sleep.

After just a few seconds, the monster opened the capsule door. 'Lucky for you I want you alive.' He pulled me out and threw me over his shoulder. 'Don't ever try a trick like that again, Victor.'

13

The Ultimatum

The monster carried me outside, saying 'The sun will warm you up.'

He climbed Mont Blanc with me over his shoulder. The speed of his ascent was incredible. Truly, I had created a superhuman being.

When we reached the summit, he put me down. We were so high above the Alps that I felt a sense of vertigo.

Even at this altitude, there was no snow. I saw now how my own life story was a mirror image of what we have done to the planet: our technology has destroyed everything that is most precious to us.

The monster looked down at me, his body a great mass of unnatural muscles. He must have read my thoughts. 'Yes, I killed your brother and I will happily kill you too, unless you obey me.'

'What do you want from me?'

'You created me, the only one of my kind. And then you abandoned me, leaving me even more alone.' The creature looked down at the desolate landscape.

'I have been observing human society in the time since my creation. In secret, of course – for some reason, the sight of me seems to frighten people.' The monster's face contorted horribly. I think he was trying to smile.

'You will create for me a female of my own kind. Someone who will not be disgusted when she looks at me. She will be my wife.'

'No! Never!'

'Why should I, alone of all the creatures in the world, have no companion?' he asked.

'Nothing will make me repeat my error,' I said.

'Create a mate for me and we will TransPod ourselves to the planet Gliese 581c, leaving your kind in peace forever.'

'But Gliese is far hotter than Earth!'

'Exactly,' he answered. 'Heat is good. It is cold

that I cannot tolerate – which is why I disliked your trick so much.'

Maybe the cold reminded him too much of when he was dead.

I considered his proposal. 'Very well. I will do what you ask.'

The monster smiled in satisfaction. 'In exactly a year I will visit you at your Institute. My bride will be ready for me – or you will know the full force of my anger.'

14

The Funeral

Billy's funeral was terrible. Sadness and guilt battled within me. I couldn't speak. I couldn't even cry. I was afraid that if I gave into my feelings I would be destroyed.

Elizabeth could see my unhappiness. But there was nothing she could say. It didn't matter. Her gentle eyes said it all.

'You're such a good friend to me, Elizabeth. Better than I merit.'

'I want to be more than your friend, Victor.'

'Elizabeth... I wish...'

'What?'

'I wish life was so simple,' I said. 'I wish we could be more than friends. I wish we could get married. Have children of our own.'

'Then why can't it happen, Victor?'

I looked over to where Dad was sitting, a broken man. How could I think about my own happiness?

'Maybe one day. But there are things I have to do first. I'm sorry.'

15

Bride of the Creature

I returned to my work. It seemed the only way to free the world of the danger I had created, but I also admit that the technical challenge fascinated me.

I wanted to see if I could control the secondary effects of the reanimation process, so that the female would not be as hideous as my first creation.

The year passed rapidly. By its end, the female creature was assembled in my laboratory at the Future Life Institute.

At about midnight, the security cameras picked up a gigantic figure circling the building.

I went to the front entrance and let the monster in.

'She's beautiful!' he said as he looked at the female I had created for him.

It was then that I realised my mistake. How could she ever love the hideous creature standing over her?

'She's *too* beautiful for you!' I said. 'When I bring her to life, she will not consent to be your bride! What if she refuses to leave Earth with you?'

I took a laser scalpel and set it to full power, cutting the female's inanimate body into pieces.

I was about to do the same to the monster when he picked me up, shouting 'You will pay for this!' and threw me against the wall, knocking me unconscious.

When I woke up, he was gone, taking the head of the female creature with him.

Somehow, I knew exactly where he was going.

16

The Creature's Fury

There was a sinister silence when I entered the living quarters upstairs.

I found my father in his study, asleep over his desk. I touched his shoulder to wake him. But he wasn't asleep. He was dead.

My whole body went icy cold, as if I had once again been plunged into one of our cryonic capsules. I wanted to cry out in horror, but found I had lost my voice.

And, somehow, I knew there was worse to come.

Elizabeth was in her room, lying on her bed. The gigantic handprints around her neck told me she was dead too.

The icy feeling was gone. In its place, a wave of hot rage consumed me.

52

The monster stepped forwards out of the shadows. He was still holding the head of the female creature.

'What have you done?' I cried. 'My father... Elizabeth... they did you no harm! Why kill them?'

'I didn't intend to kill your father,' he admitted. 'I just told him about how you created me. And that I had killed your brother. I didn't know you could kill a man by words alone. How fragile you humans are!'

'You broke his heart,' I cried. 'But why Elizabeth? What possible reason was there to kill her?'

'You will put this head on her body – and bring her back to life.' He held the head out to me. I had no choice but to take it from him.

Then the monster turned to my darling Elizabeth. He placed both his hands on her neck and pulled. I watched him tear her beautiful head from her body.

Screaming in horror, I dropped the head I was holding and ran from the room. I ran to my father's TransPod and programmed it for the North Pole:

the coldest place left on Earth, a place where perhaps the monster would not follow me.

But just as the TransPod took off, the creature jumped onto it. He was too heavy for the machine. Inevitably, it spiralled out of control, crashing near Trondheim in Norway.

Thankfully, it seemed the monster had fallen off during the short flight. Unfortunately, the TransPod no longer functioned. Instead, I bought a small boat in Trondheim and continued north by sea.

On the third day I saw a small black spot in the water behind me. 'No!' I cried.

It was the monster, swimming after me at superhuman speed.

17

Man's Last Hope

As we raced North, I saw humanity's final, desperate attempt to stop the process of global warming and cool the Earth: hundreds of ships, projecting great columns of water vapour into the atmosphere. All of them controlled by computers.

It was a strange, unearthly vision. So many ships and not one human to be seen. I had never felt so alone.

The monster was getting closer. I could see his face in the water now. Tied onto his back was the headless body of Elizabeth.

It was then that I heard a human voice shout: 'Ahoy! Do you require assistance?'

A maintenance ship had seen me. It was a much larger, faster boat than mine – if I could persuade the crew to take me North, maybe I had a chance of escaping the monster. I came alongside their ship, and they lowered a ladder* so that I could climb on board.

'Do you see that?' I pointed to the creature in the water.

'Good God!' the Captain gasped. 'Is that a man swimming?'

'Not a man. A monster. I don't have time to explain, but the further north we get, the safer we will be.'

'We have to rescue him,' the Captain said.

'No! You don't understand!'

The creature was approaching the ship, but I ran to detach the ladder so that he couldn't climb on board.

'Are you mad?' the Captain shouted as the ladder dropped into the water.

*ladder: *une échelle*

Suddenly there was a loud banging sound and the ship began to rock dangerously. A moment later the monster's head appeared over the side of the ship. Somehow he had managed to climb up.

As the sailors looked on in horror, he pulled himself on board and threw Elizabeth's headless body onto the deck. From a sack, he produced the head of the female creature.

'You know what you must do, Victor,' he said.

'This is insane.' I heard a strange, broken sound. I realised it was my own laughter. 'There is only one thing I must do, and that is to make sure that no one ever repeats my mistake.'

I ran to the Emergency station, knowing it would contain a flare gun* to signal for help. Before the creature had time to react, I took the gun and held it to my head.

And as I squeeze the trigger, I pray to God for forgiveness...

---

*flare gun: *pistolet d'alarme*

Captain's Log, Maintenance Ship 'Shelley'

This record of the extraordinary life of the man called Victor Frankenstein was found on a BiblioFile implant we recovered from the body after his suicide.

We believe it was Frankenstein's intention to destroy the implant by shooting himself with the flare gun, but if so he was not successful.

I will add the following few words.

After Frankenstein killed himself with the ship's flare gun, the monster he had created let out an indescribable cry of suffering. He took the flare gun from the dead man's hand, reloaded it and placed the barrel in his mouth.

His head exploded in a fireball and his gigantic, burning body dropped over the side of the ship.

As we watched, a large black shape began to rise from the darkness until a burned, half-destroyed head broke the surface of the water. To our horror, we saw the monster start to swim once again.

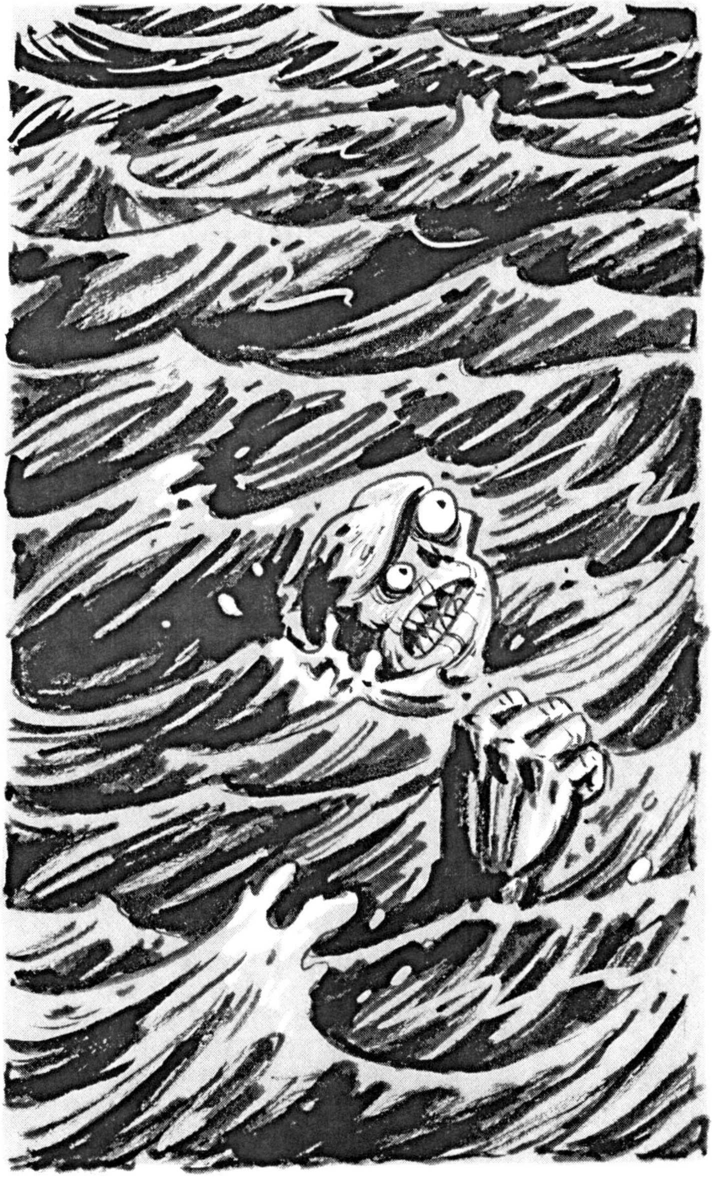

Non, les classiques ne sont pas intouchables : la preuve, c'est *Crazy Classics* !

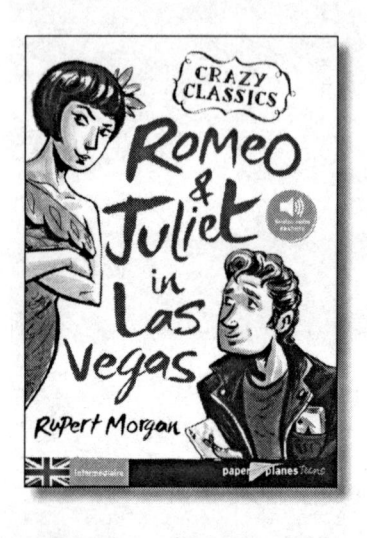

Romeo & Juliet in Las Vegas
Roger Morris
Illustré par Euan Cook

Lorsque Romeo Montague et Juliet Capulet, descendants de familles mafieuses rivales, se rencontrent et tombent éperdument amoureux, les problèmes surgissent... La tragédie de Shakespeare change de décor : nous sommes à Las Vegas en 1979, avec Juliet, Romeo et... Elvis Presley !

Macbeth and the Creature from Hell
Roger Morris
Illustré par Euan Cook

Lorsque trois affreuses sorcières rencontrent le valeureux Lord Macbeth sur la lande envahie de brume, elles font cette prophétie : « un jour, tu seras roi d'Écosse ». Mais lorsque le diable s'en mêle, rien ne se passe comme prévu. La tragédie de Shakespeare est réinventée : magie noire, trahisons, meurtres... et une sale bestiole !

Ce ne sont pas des livres d'histoire ordinaires. C'est *Terrible Times*. On vous aura prévenus !

Bubonic Britain
Philippa Boston
Illustré par Mark Beech

Tout commence avec une puce... qui grimpe sur un rat... qui grimpe sur un navire... Un an plus tard, la moitié de l'Angleterre succombe à la Grande Peste de 1348. *Bubonic Britain* vous plonge dans Londres ravagée par l'épidémie, puis dans le récit de Bella, adolescente anglaise qui se bat contre la Mort Noire.

Deadly Jobs
Philippa Boston
Illustré par Mark Beech

Il n'est pas si lointain le temps où seuls quelques enfants pouvaient aller à l'école... Les autres, parfois dès 4 ans, étaient ramoneurs ou travaillaient à la mine...
Deadly Jobs vous plonge dans la terrible Angleterre du XIXe siècle et dans le récit de Tom, un jeune anglais qui, en 1832, tente simplement de rester en vie.

paper planes *teens*

C'est aussi un site :

www.paperplanesteens.fr

- Plonge-toi dans l'histoire en écoutant la **version audio** !

- Retrouve **toutes les infos** sur l'actualité de la collection (auteurs, illustrateurs, nouveautés, événements...)